To Maria & Karly—sisters always.
—C. F.

To all my sisters, thank you. No matter our differences or how great our disagreements,
you made sure that your love for me was never in doubt. Thank you for supporting me
and my dreams, in my darkest and brightest of days.
—B. J.

Running Press Kids
Hachette Book Group
1290 Avenue of the Americas, New York, NY 10104
www.runningpress.com/rpkids
@RP_Kids

Printed in China

First Edition: June 2022

Published by Running Press Kids, an imprint of Perseus Books, LLC, a subsidiary of Hachette Book Group, Inc.
The Running Press Kids name and logo is a trademark of the Hachette Book Group.

The Hachette Speakers Bureau provides a wide range of authors for speaking events.
To find out more, go to www.hachettespeakersbureau.com or call (866) 376-6591.

The publisher is not responsible for websites (or their content) that are not owned by the publisher.

Print book cover and interior design by Frances J. Soo Ping Chow.

Library of Congress Cataloging-in-Publication Data:
Names: Finison, Carrie, author. | Jackson, Bea, illustrator.
Title: Lulu and Zoey : a sister story / written by Carrie Finison; illustrated by Brittany Jackson.
Description: First edition. | Philadelphia : Running Press Kids, 2022. | Audience: Ages 4-8.
Identifiers: LCCN 2021020745 (print) | LCCN 2021020746 (ebook) | ISBN 9780762473984 (hardcover) |
ISBN 9780762473977 (ebook) | ISBN 9780762474134 (ebook) | ISBN 9780762474141 (kindle edition)
Subjects: LCSH: African American girls—Juvenile fiction. | Sisters—Juvenile fiction. | Picture books for children. |
CYAC: Stories in rhyme. | Sisters—Fiction. | African Americans—Fiction. | LCGFT: Picture books.
Classification: LCC PZ8.3.F623 Lu 2022 (print) | LCC PZ8.3.F623 (ebook) | DDC 813.6 [E]—dc23
LC record available at https://lccn.loc.gov/2021020745
LC ebook record available at https://lccn.loc.gov/2021020746

ISBNs: 978-0-7624-7398-4 (hardcover), 978-0-7624-7397-7 (ebook),
978-0-7624-7413-4 (ebook), 978-0-7624-7414-1 (ebook)

1010

10 9 8 7 6 5 4 3 2 1

Sometimes Lulu wants to play.
But Zoey doesn't. "Not today."

Sometimes Zoey hides her book
when Lulu only wants to look.

Sometimes Zoey
has the best.

Sometimes Lulu
grabs THE REST.

Sometimes Zoey tries to share,
and that's when Lulu won't play fair.

Sometimes Lulu decorates,
and that's what Zoey really HATES!

Sometimes sisters play too rough.

Then Aunt Eliza says,
"ENOUGH!"

Sometimes angry sisters SHOUT,
and STOMP,

and SLAM,

SLAM

and sulk,
and pout.

Sometimes sisters, each alone,

enjoy the quiet on their own.

They draw,

they paint,

they rest,

they write . . .
until they both forget the fight.

Sometimes sisters open doors
to share their dreams
of distant shores.

And then they write and illustrate
a story that they both create—

of mermaid friends, dolphin flips,
and sunken pirate treasure ships.

Sometimes Lulu adds some art
but DOESN'T draw on Zoey's part.

Sometimes Zoey adds a line,
and Lulu DOESN'T say, "That's mine!"

They still have
chapter two to make,

but first they take
a cookie break.

Sometimes sisters grab the best,

break off half,
and share the rest.

Sometimes they fight.

Sometimes they're friends.
A sister story never ends.

Always, sisters have each other.
And sometimes sisters have . . .

another!